MY HORSE
Coloring Book

JOHN GREEN

Introduction and Captions by
CANDACE WARD

DOVER PUBLICATIONS, INC.
New York

Bibliographical Note

My Horse Coloring Book is a new work, first published by Dover Publications, Inc., in 1994.

DOVER *Pictorial Archive* SERIES

This book belongs to the Dover Pictorial Archive Series. You may use the designs and illustrations for graphics and crafts applications, free and without special permission, provided that you include no more than four in the same publication or project. (For permission for additional use, please write to Dover Publications, Inc., 180 Varick Street, New York, NY 10014.)

However, republication or reproduction of any illustration by any other graphic service, whether it be in a book or in any other design resource, is strictly prohibited.

International Standard Book Number: 0-486-28064-0

Manufactured in the United States of America
Dover Publications, Inc., 31 East 2nd Street, Mineola, N.Y. 11501

INTRODUCTION

F OR THOUSANDS OF YEARS, the horse has held a fascination for humans; its presence in mythology, art and romance gives testimony to its special place in the human imagination. But the first horse was very different from the animal that has come to epitomize nobility and grace.

The animal that we recognize today as the horse evolved from one of the earliest mammals, *Hyracotherium* or *Eohippus* (the Dawn Horse), which first appeared around 55 million years ago. These animals were quite small—only about 12 inches high—and instead of hooves had four toes on the front feet and three on the back. These four-toed animals gradually evolved into the three-toed "horses" that appeared around 38 million years ago. By this time their size had increased slightly and by the time the three-toed animals disappeared, they had evolved from browsers, subsisting on a leafy diet, to grass-eaters. One-toed horses, which succeeded the three-toed grazers, first appeared about 15 million years ago, and the one-toed *Dinohippus* was the apparent ancestor of the genus known as *Equus*—the same to which the modern horse belongs. The earliest evidence of human contact with the horse suggests that the animal was first hunted for food, and it is uncertain where or when the horse was first domesticated, or whether it was first used to ride or drive. By 3000 B.C., however, it is certain that many different peoples in Asia, Europe and North Africa were using the horse for both purposes.

From the beginning, man's relationship with the horse has been based on utility; the horse has enabled man to hunt more efficiently, to fight more effectively and to labor more productively. With increased industrialization and mechanization, however, this relationship has shifted. While the horse still functions as a work animal in many parts of the world, in the United States and the United Kingdom its primary function is to provide pleasure. Though people have always enjoyed horseback riding, it was only in this century that the horse was not the primary means of transport, thereby making equitation an activity of choice rather than necessity.

My Horse Coloring Book focuses on this more recent phase of our relationship with the horse. In the following pages young readers can learn about some of the responsibilities of caring for a horse or pony and also about the pleasures to be derived from good horsemanship. The book contains a brief introduction to the horse's anatomy and basic information on the care of horses (stabling, feeding, grooming, etc.), their training and riding.

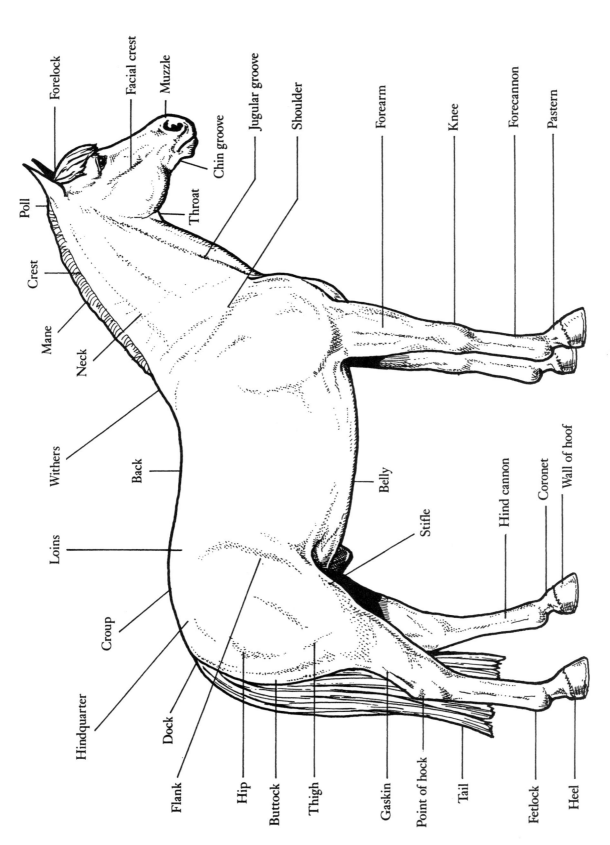

Points of the horse. A knowledge of the points, or physical characteristics, of the horse is crucial to good horsemanship. Not only does this knowledge help a person when purchasing a horse, but also in riding and caring for the animal. This drawing shows the main points of the horse. The most important of these are the points of the legs and feet, since locomotion is the horse's primary attribute. Correct conformation, or how well a horse conforms to certain physical standards, assures the prospective buyer that the horse is in good physical condition, able to withstand the work and strains involved in normal exercise.

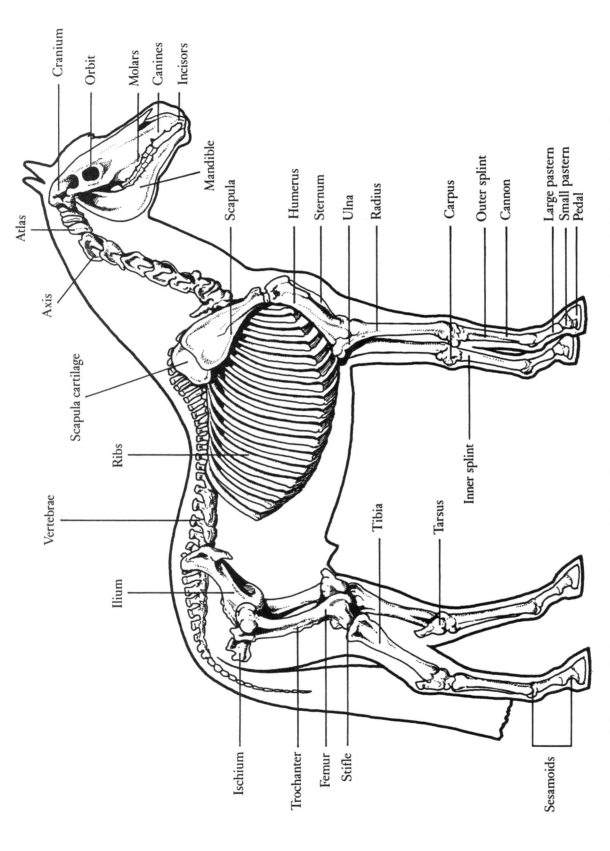

Cranium
Orbit
Molars
Canines
Incisors
Atlas
Mandible
Axis
Scapula
Scapula cartilage
Humerus
Sternum
Ulna
Radius
Ribs
Carpus
Outer splint
Cannon
Large pastern
Small pastern
Pedal
Vertebrae
Ilium
Inner splint
Tibia
Tarsus
Ischium
Trochanter
Femur
Stifle
Sesamoids

Skeleton of the horse. In a normal adult horse, there are 205 bones in addition to small amounts of cartilage. Notice the long bones of the legs, which pivot on pulley-like joints to restrict movement to front and back. The horse's hock, consisting of a series of joints bound together by ligaments, is the main propelling force of the horse, allowing it to gallop and jump. In addition to providing anchorage for the muscles and ligaments, the bones store calcium and phosphorus; bone marrow produces red and white corpuscles.

5

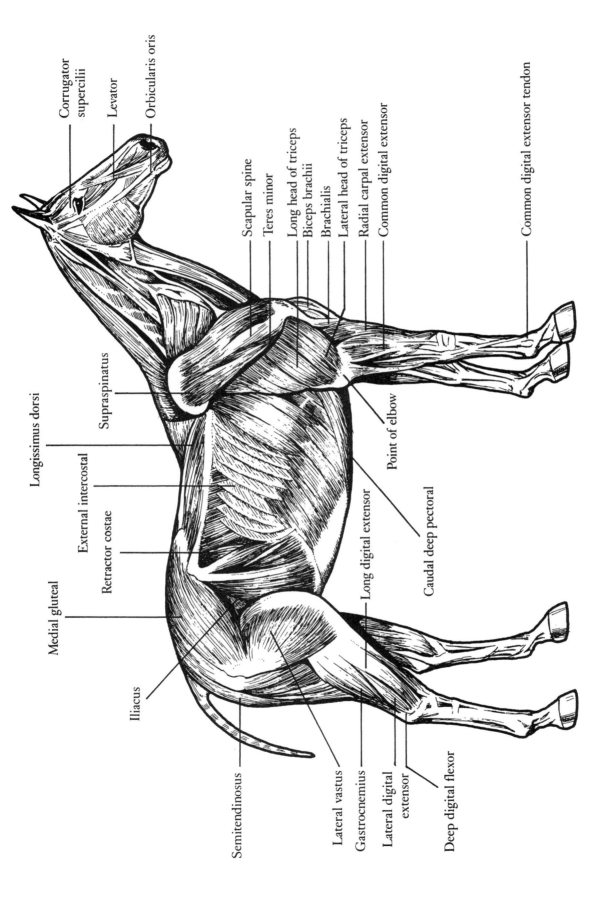

Corrugator supercilii

Levator

Orbicularis oris

Scapular spine

Teres minor

Long head of triceps

Biceps brachii

Brachialis

Lateral head of triceps

Radial carpal extensor

Common digital extensor

Common digital extensor tendon

Longissimus dorsi

Supraspinatus

External intercostal

Retractor costae

Medial gluteal

Iliacus

Point of elbow

Long digital extensor

Caudal deep pectoral

Semitendinosus

Lateral vastus

Gastrocnemius

Lateral digital extensor

Deep digital flexor

Principal muscles of the horse. The muscles of the horse allow the animal to move and maintain its posture. As mentioned earlier, these muscles are attached to skeletal bones. The illustration here shows how the leg muscles are concentrated at the top of the limbs. Because the bottom bones and joints are connected only by tendons, which transfer the muscle contraction to them, this part of the horse is very susceptible to injury. The foreleg is unusual in that it is attached to the horse's upper body only by muscles and ligaments, which prevents excessive shock to the spine by absorbing the force of the impact when the animal jumps or gallops.

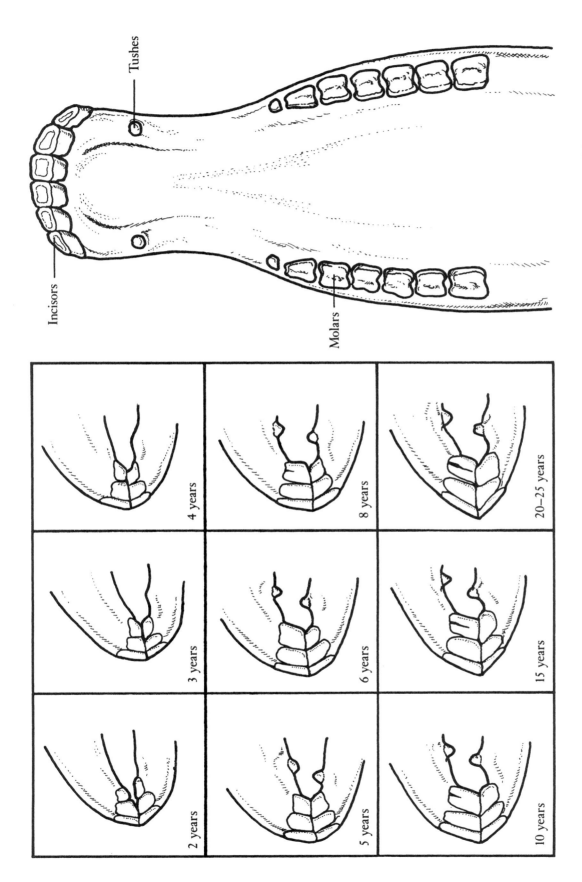

The jaw of the horse; how to tell the horse's age. The drawing on the right shows the kind of teeth a horse has on each jaw: the molars are used to grind food while the incisors are for biting. While male horses always have two canine teeth (sometimes called tushes) on the top and bottom jaw, sometimes female horses grow canine teeth as well. When a horse's age is not known, it can be estimated by examining its teeth. As shown here, the horse's teeth

change as it grows older. Between the ages of one and five, for example, the horse's temporary incisors will be replaced by permanent ones. After the age of eight or nine, a groove appears on the upper corner incisors called Galvayne's Groove. As the horse ages, the groove gradually extends down the tooth—at age 15 it reaches about halfway down the tooth and at age 20 it reaches the bottom; it then begins to disappear at the top, and by the age of 30, it will be gone.

7

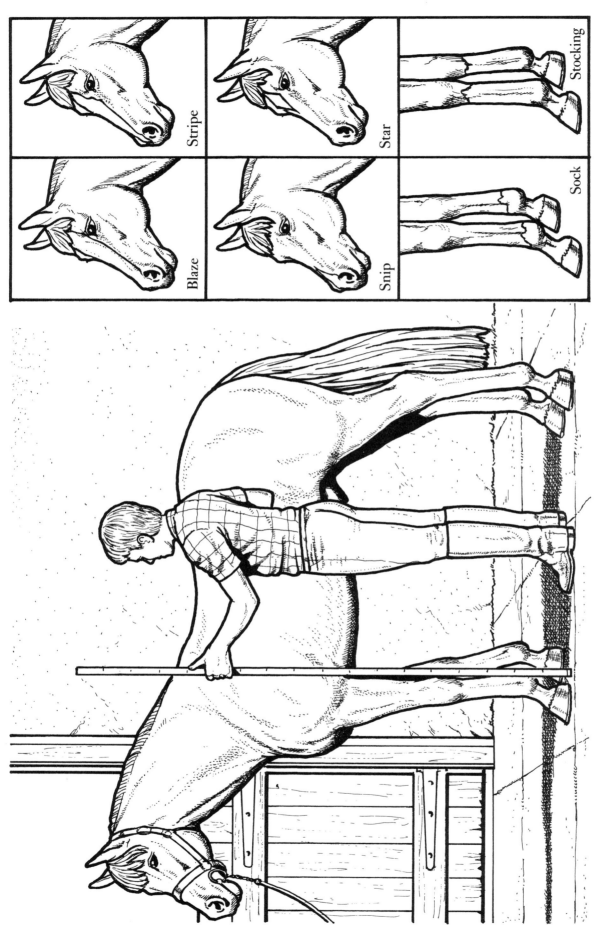

Stripe

Star

Stocking

Blaze

Snip

Sock

The height of the horse and general markings. The primitive horse most likely measured about 12 hands; to-day horses stand anywhere from 20 to 14.2 hands high, depending on the breed. Horses under 14.2 hands high are designated ponies. One "hand," originally the distance across a man's knuckles, is equal to 4 inches or 10.16 centimeters; the abbreviation "hh" means "hands high." Horses' heights are measured from the highest point of the withers to the ground. In addition to their height, horses also have several kinds of facial markings by which they can be identified. The markings shown here are a blaze, stripe, snip and star. Among the various types of leg markings are socks, which cover the fetlock and part of the cannon, and stockings, which extend farther up the leg to the knee or hock.

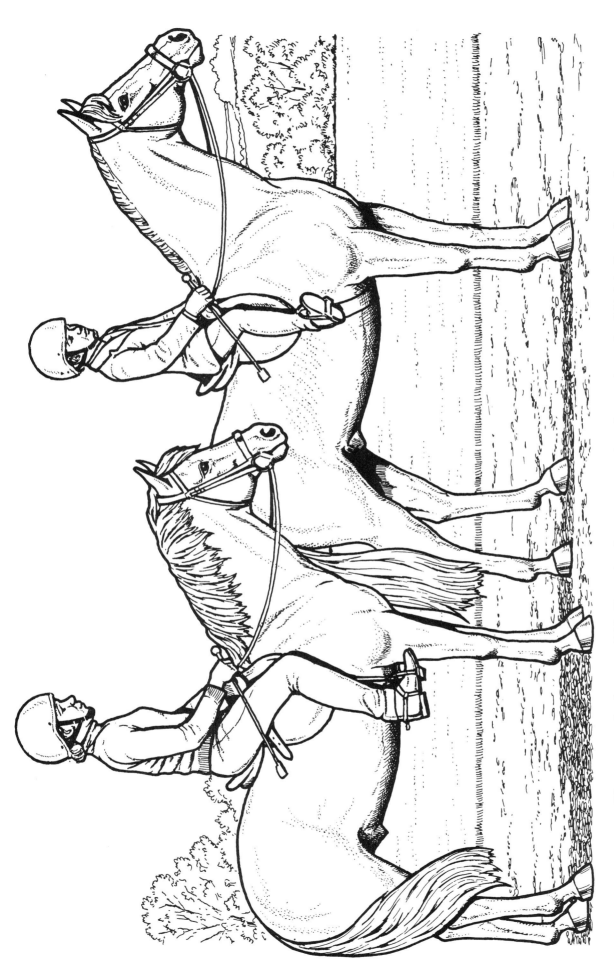

The correct-sized mount. This illustration shows two riders on mounts of the wrong size; the rider on the left is on a horse that is too small, while the other rider's horse is too large. Choosing a mount that is the right size for the rider is extremely important, especially when those riders are beginners or children. For example, if a child is mounted on a large horse, his feet may not contact the horse where they can be used as "aids," the lines of communication from rider to horse; in other words, the rider's legs are used to control the horse's movements, but they can only be used effectively if the point of contact with the horse is the correct one. A general rule to follow is, if the soles of the rider's feet are in line with the bottom of the horse's belly, the mount is the correct size.

9

American Shetland

Connemara

New Forest

Welsh

Hafflinger

Ten popular breeds of ponies for the young rider.
When some people hear the word "pony," they automatically picture the familiar Shetland. However, a pony is any horse under 14.2 hh; at 12–14 hh, the New Forest breed, though designated a pony, is much larger than the Shetland, which averages 9.3 hh. At one time, most of these

Pony of the Americas

Shetland

Iceland

Highland

Exmoor

ponies were bred for hard work: the Shetland was bred to work in the coal mines during the nineteenth century and the Hafflinger, a Tyrolese breed, was used as a pack and draught horse in the agricultural and forestry industries of its native mountains. Today, however, these ponies are primarily used as suitable mounts for young riders because of their size, sturdiness and disposition.

Buying a horse or pony. There are two very important things to remember when buying a horse or pony—make sure you know what to look for in a horse, or take someone with you who knows about horses. Usually, horses are purchased at one of two places, a breeding farm or a horse dealer's stable. Regardless of where you buy your animal, you should always ride the horse first, under as many different conditions as you can; if possible, take a veter- inarian with you to determine the soundness of the horse, or obtain a veterinarian's certificate of health from the seller. It is also a good idea to make arrangements for the return of the animal if there is a problem. Perhaps the most important thing to remember when looking for a horse or pony is to take your time; buying a horse is an important decision and should not be rushed.

Keeping horses at grass. If horses are not stabled, they can be kept at grass—that is, kept in a pasture during clement weather and then stabled at night or during extreme weather conditions. There are advantages and disadvantages to keeping a horse at grass. For example, grass is the horse's natural food and is full of vitamins. However, grass also contains a lot of water and must often be supplemented with other grains, especially after the summer months. The field must be properly maintained, with secure gates and fences, an adequate fresh water supply and a shelter to protect the horse from the wind, rain and sun.

Catching your horse, the correct way. Horses are by nature friendly animals, and dislike being left by themselves. Even so, sometimes they can be difficult to catch in the field. In such cases, there are several ways to train your horse to come to you. For example, when you enter the pasture, be sure to have a treat—an apple, carrot or some oats in a pail—with which to reward the animal when he does come to you. It's best to do this a number of times, even when you don't need to catch the horse, since he will then get accustomed to coming when you call or whistle. Whatever you do, don't try to catch your horse by chasing him—he's much faster than you and will only be frightened by such an approach.

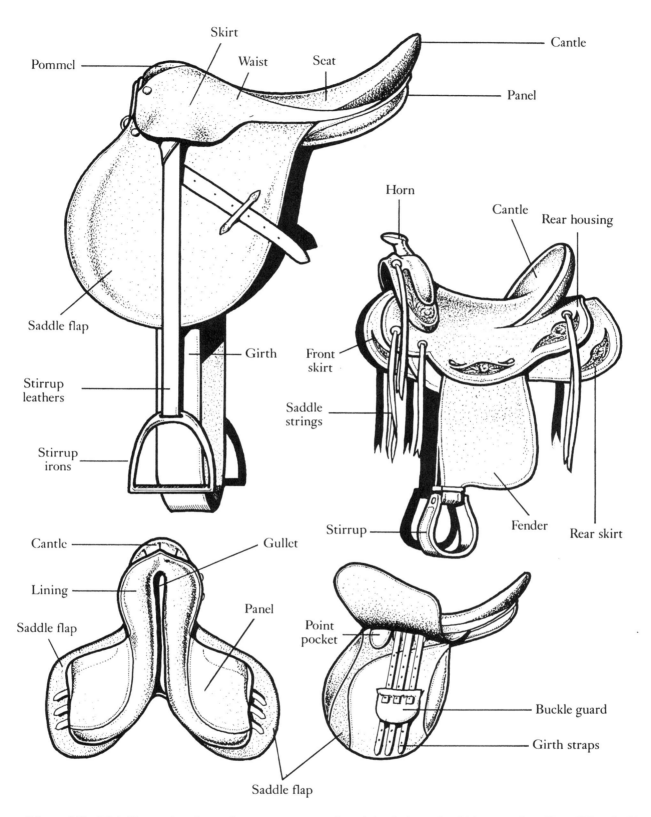

Pommel Skirt Waist Seat Cantle Panel

Saddle flap Girth

Stirrup leathers

Stirrup irons

Horn Cantle Rear housing

Front skirt

Saddle strings

Stirrup Fender Rear skirt

Cantle Gullet

Lining

Saddle flap Panel

Point pocket

Buckle guard

Girth straps

Saddle flap

Parts of the saddle. This illustration shows the two types of saddle most commonly used for riding, the English saddle and the Western. All saddles are constructed on a framework called a tree, which determines the saddle's final shape. Over the tree there are layers of webbing, canvas, serge and leather; the pad, which rests on the horse's back, is made of felt or wool stuffing. When looking for a saddle to purchase—either new or used—there are several things to consider: the style of riding, the size of the rider and the fit of the saddle. The last consideration is perhaps the most important because a poorly fitted saddle will make both the horse and rider uncomfortable.

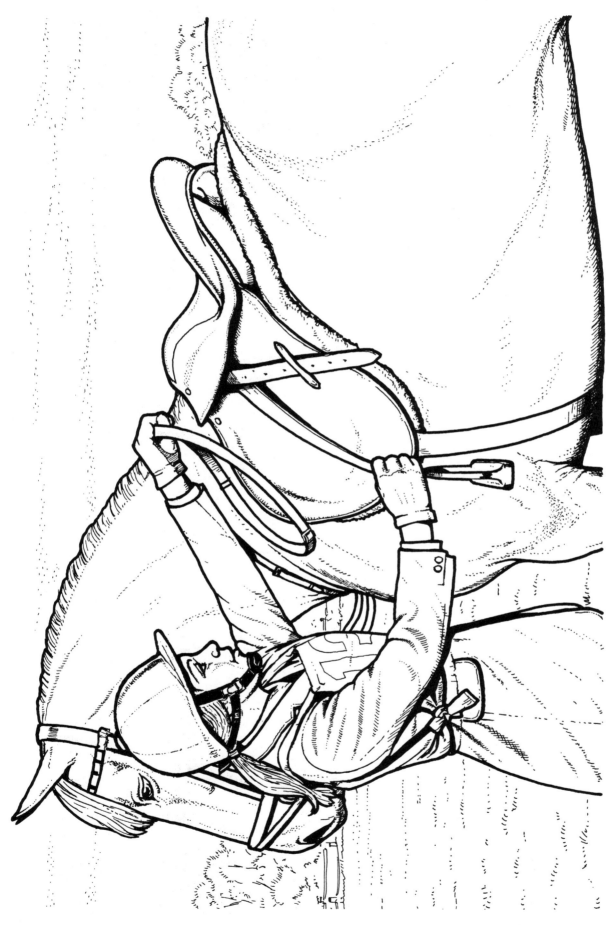

English, or all-purpose, saddle. There are many different types of saddle, all designed with certain kinds of work or riding in mind. The English, or all-purpose, or flat, saddle is comprised of a variety of types as well, such as the "park" or hacking saddle, the "forward-seat" or jumping saddle and the racing saddle. These saddles have a flat seat and are used for pleasure riding, polo, racing, jumping and showing. The advantage of the English saddle is its relatively light weight and comfort to both horse and rider. There is no horn or high cantle, as on a Western saddle, and the rider's position is not restricted.

Western saddle and Western-style riding. Western saddles were developed for specific tasks, such as herding and roping cattle. The most conspicuous differences between the Western saddle and the English type are the saddle horn and the high cantle of the former. The lariat used in roping cattle is attached to the horn, and the blanket roll is fastened to the cantle. The stirrups on the Western saddle are different as well, being wooden rather than iron, and covered to protect the rider's legs. Stirrups are usually set so that the rider's legs are almost straight rather than bent at the knee. Also, when riding Western style, the rider does not "post" or rise to the trot as when riding English.

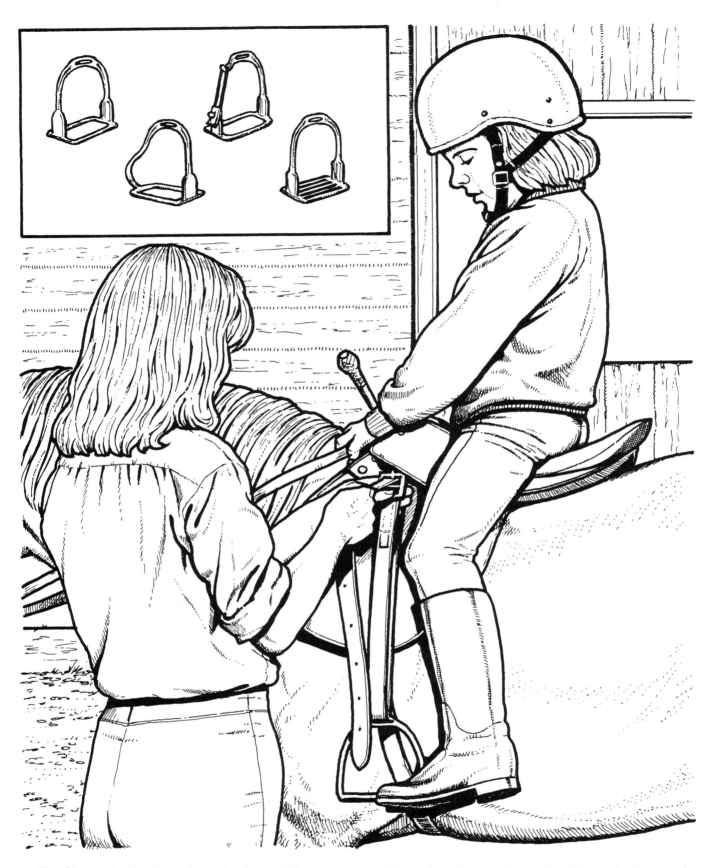

Checking and adjusting stirrup leathers. Riders sometimes ride without the use of stirrups—when, for example, intermediate riders ride bareback to acquire greater balance and a firmer seat. Most often, though, riders work with the stirrups, which are adjusted after the rider is in the saddle. As mentioned before, stirrups are adjusted to different lengths according to the riding style. Because the correct seat in the English style requires a bent knee, the stirrup leathers are adjusted higher. To measure the correct length, the rider should take his feet out of the stirrups; adjust the stirrup leathers so that the stirrup irons are even with the inside ankle bone.

18

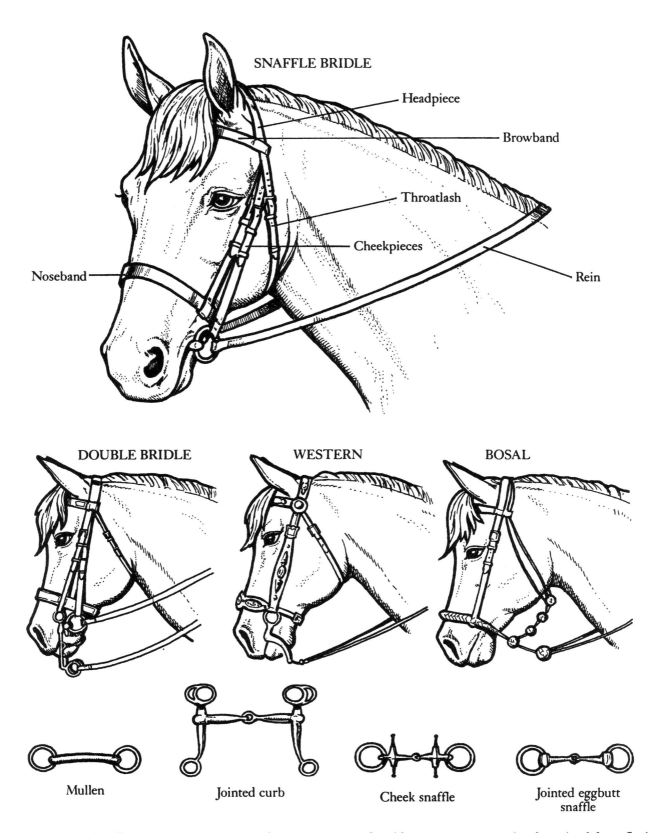

SNAFFLE BRIDLE

Headpiece

Browband

Throatlash

Cheekpieces

Noseband

Rein

DOUBLE BRIDLE   WESTERN   BOSAL

Mullen   Jointed curb   Cheek snaffle   Jointed eggbutt
snaffle

The parts of the bridle. The top picture shows the parts of a bridle with one of the simplest and most commonly used bits, the snaffle bit. This bit consists of a straight or jointed piece of metal (the mouthpiece), with rings at both ends for the reins. The other parts of the bridle are the noseband, the headpiece, the browband, the throatlash, the cheekpieces and the reins. The bridle should fit the horse comfortably, so as not to restrict the animal from flexing his jaws and breathing freely. Three other types of bridle are the double bridle, used only by experienced riders, the Western bridle and the bosal; some other types of bits include the mullen and the jointed-curb, as well as the types of snaffle bit shown here.

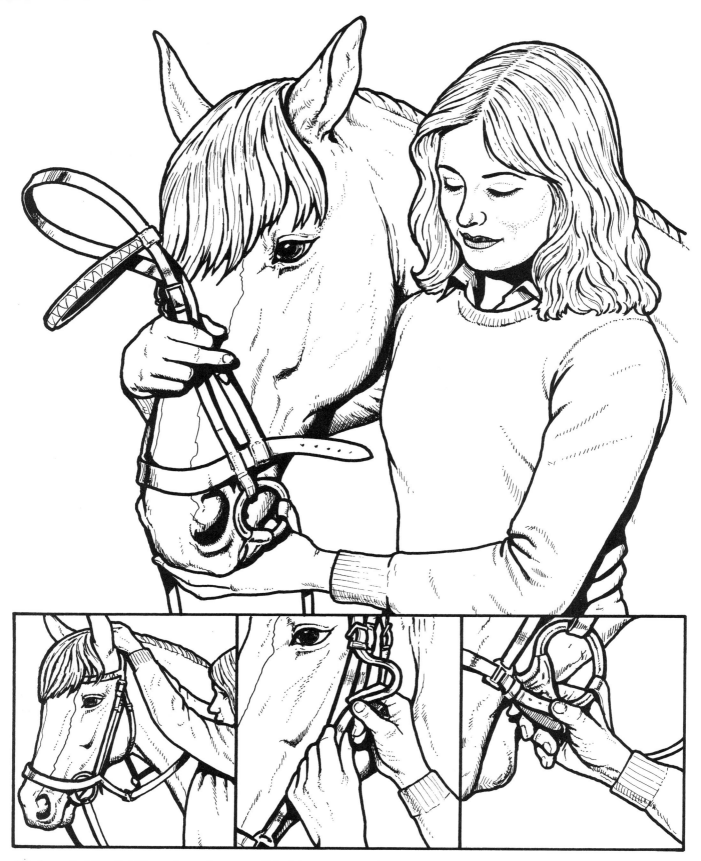

Fitting a bridle. Bridling a horse is accomplished in several steps. First, approach the horse's left side either from behind or from the side. (If you try to bridle a horse from directly in front, he will back away.) Holding the reins in the right hand and the headpiece in the left, slip the reins over the horse's head and neck. Transfer the headpiece to the right hand, holding it as shown, and hold the bit with the thumb and forefinger of the left hand. Slip the bit into the horse's mouth and then use both hands to slip the headpiece over the ears, one at a time. Fasten the throatlash and noseband.

Cleaning tack. Keeping your tack—harness, saddle, bridle and other equipment—clean and in good repair is as important as good grooming. Tack should be cleaned daily, usually after the horse is exercised. The saddle and other leather should be wiped with a damp sponge and saddle soap; if necessary, mud and dried sweat can be scrubbed off first with a brush or a wet sponge, using plenty of soap. Rinse the leather, but don't saturate it, and then dry it with a chamois leather. When dry, apply saddle soap with a damp sponge and work it into the leather without creating a lather. After the saddle has absorbed the soap, go over it with a moist sponge. Lastly, wipe the saddle once more with the chamois leather. The metal pieces of tack—the bit, stirrup irons, etc.—can be cleaned with metal polish. Before or after the actual cleaning, go over all your equipment for signs of wear.

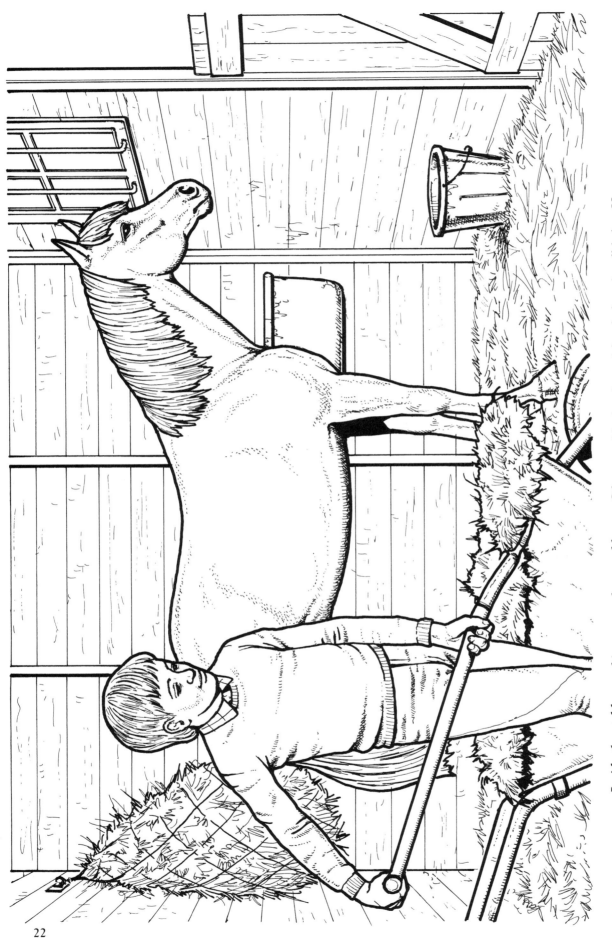

Inside the stable, mucking out and general layout. Of the two kinds of stabling most common today—the straight stall and the loose box—the latter is preferable in many ways. First, it allows the horse more freedom of movement, which is important since many horses spend much of their day in them. The ideal size for a loose box is about 12' × 12' for a horse that stands 14.3 to 16.2 hh. It should, of course, be built of quality materials. Keeping a

stable clean is crucial to the horse's well-being. Here we see a young rider "mucking out" the stable, or cleaning out the manure and old straw, a task usually done the first thing in the morning before laying the "day bed" of fresh straw. Notice that the horse's hay is placed in a haynet securely attached to a bolt ring at a level that allows the horse to feed comfortably. The water bucket is placed at the opposite end of the box to help keep the water clean.

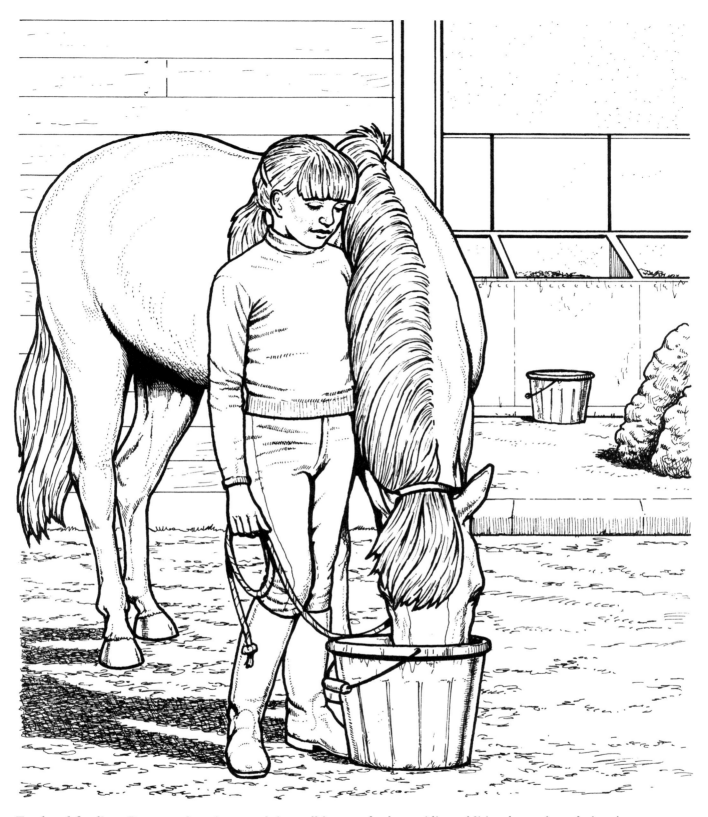

Feed and feeding. Because a horse's stomach is small in proportion to its body, it should be fed relatively small amounts often rather than large amounts only once or twice a day. The amount and type of food a horse needs depends on its size and the kind of work it does. Horse food falls into the two broad categories: bulk food (grass or hay) and concentrates (grains such as oats, corn, barley and bran). Concentrated foods supplement the horse's diet of bulk food, providing additional protein and vitamins as necessary. Once you've determined the combination of bulk and concentrated food that is correct for your horse, it is also important to establish and maintain a feeding schedule. Remember that most horses feed better at night, and so should receive the greatest portion of food at the last feed of the day.

At the blacksmith's. The art of the blacksmith, or farrier, is difficult to learn and requires diligence, strength and, of course, a thorough knowledge of horses. Because the horse's feet are so important to his performance and his health, they need to be regularly checked by a blacksmith, even if the horse is unshod. In this illustration, the black-

smith is hot-shoeing a horse; in the left background are the forge and the anvil where the smith heats the shoe and hammers it into shape before attaching it to the horse's foot.

As you can see, the smith has already taken off the old shoe and is now replacing it with a newly fitted one, hammering it onto the foot with the clenches his assistant hands him.

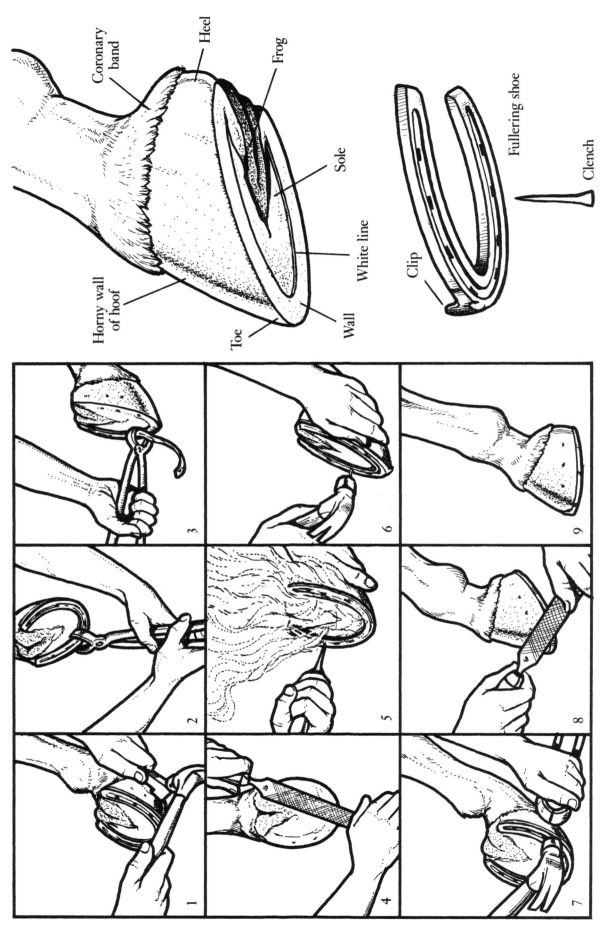

Coronary band

Heel

Frog

Sole

White line

Wall

Toe

Horny wall of hoof

Fullering shoe

Clip

Clench

Fitting a shoe and parts of the hoof. Horses that are ridden regularly on hard surfaces need to be shod. There are two methods of shoeing a horse: cold-shoeing, where pre-cast shoes are fitted to the hoof cold or, as shown here, hot-shoeing. In this method, the hot shoe is "custom-fitted" to the horse's hoof by a blacksmith or farrier. In drawings 1 through 3, the farrier removes the old shoe by cutting the old clenches and pulling off the shoe with pincers. He then trims and files the overgrown horn and fits the newly forged, still hot shoe to the hoof (drawings 4 and 5). The new shoe is attached by clenches (drawings 6 and 7), which are then filed so that they are flush with the horny wall of the hoof (drawing 8). To the right you can see the hoof and its parts, as well as a typical horseshoe and clench.

Hoof care, cleaning out hoof. The feet of the horse need to be inspected and cleaned daily; without such care, he might become lame. When picking up front and back feet, face the rear of the horse. Lean against the horse's shoulder to shift his weight to the opposite side and run your hand down the tendon to the fetlock and pull up on the hair. Cup the hoof in one hand while you use the hoof-pick to clean the sole and frog carefully. Although you should check the feet at night to remove any stones or pebbles the horse might have picked up during the day, clean out the hooves in the morning; the earth picked up when the horse is out helps keep the frog and sole moist. Applying hoof oil daily (inset) helps prevent cracks and keeps the hooves healthy.

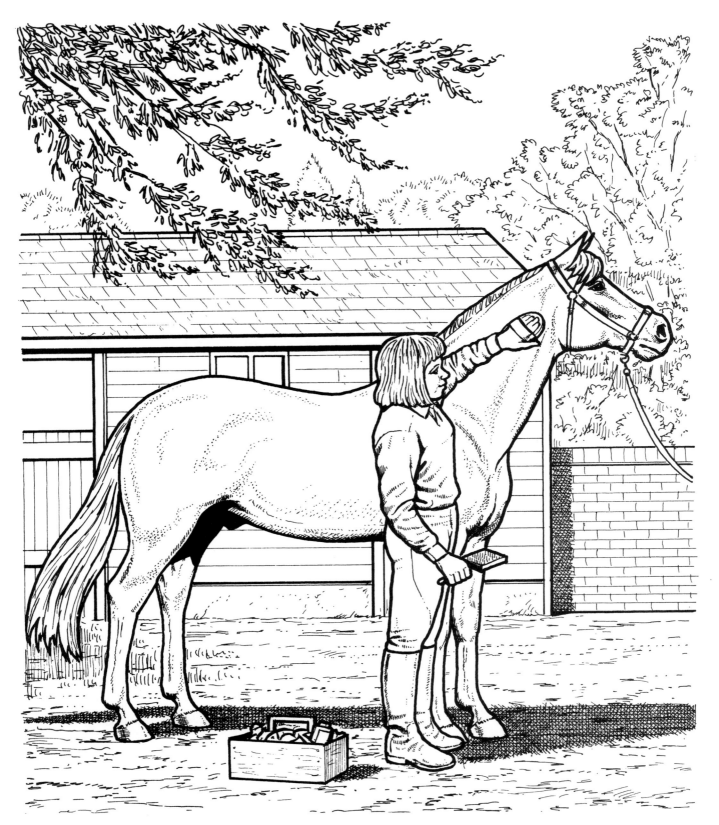

The importance of grooming. Good grooming is an essential element of horse care. Not only does a thorough grooming keep up your horse's appearance, it also massages his muscles, stimulates blood circulation and helps the horse's body make the most of his feed. Another reason to keep your horse well groomed is that you will be able to detect anything wrong with the animal more quickly— lameness or illness, for example. There are three different stages of grooming, performed at different times of the day: "quartering," usually done in the morning, before exercise; "setting fair," the last and simplest grooming of the day; and "strapping," the thorough grooming that a horse receives after being exercised and that is the most time-consuming, taking between half and three-quarters of an hour.

28

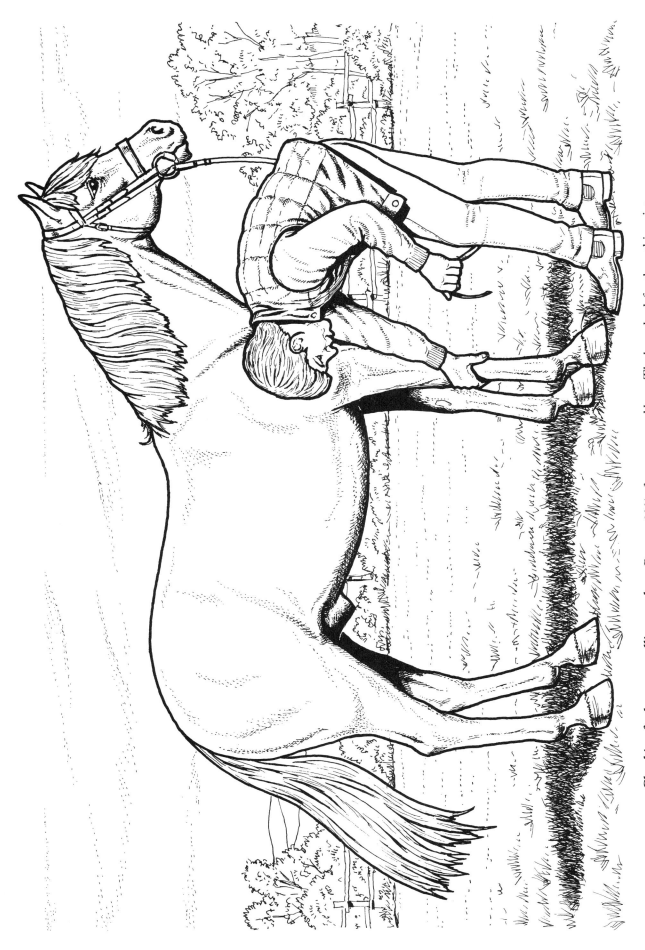

Checking for lumps, swellings on legs. Because 90% of all lameness is caused by a problem in the feet, they should be carefully inspected daily; the next place to check for lameness is the legs. To check the legs, start at the elbow or hock and run your hand down the horse's legs, feeling for any unusual lumps or swellings and checking for tenderness and heat. The best check for these things is to run your hand over the corresponding leg, especially if you think you feel heat, which can be difficult to detect. Lifting and bending the leg to check for any resistance on the horse's part also helps determine the site of possible injury or lameness.

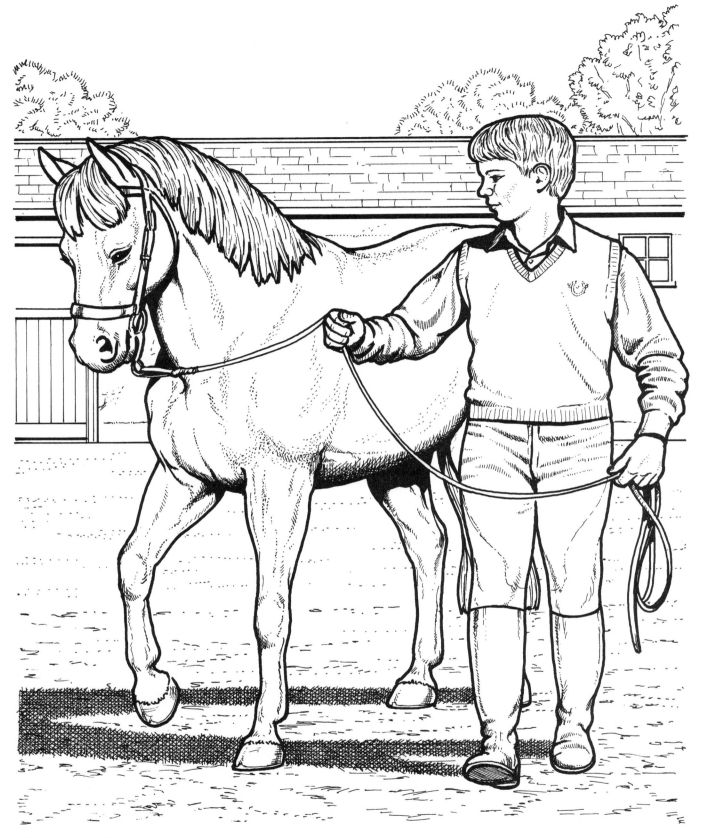

Checking your horse for lameness. If you suspect lameness, and have already checked the feet carefully, try to determine which leg the horse is favoring. Leading the horse at a slow trot is the best way to do this. If the horse is lame in one of his back legs, he will nod or duck his head when weight is placed on the lame foot; if the lameness is in front, the opposite occurs—the horse will nod when the sound leg touches the ground. After determining which leg is being favored, if an inspection of the foot and leg doesn't reveal anything, the injury may be located in the shoulder (if the horse favors a front leg) or the stifle, hip joint or spine (if he favors a rear leg).

Rugging up, use of a blanket when a horse is suffering from a cold or cough. Horses are commonly covered with a blanket after they have been clipped for the winter and are not working, or when they are suffering from a cold. Although colds are a common illness among horses, they can develop into pneumonia or a more serious illness, so a veterinarian should be consulted as soon as possible. Colds are caused by exposure, overwork or bad feeding, and they are highly contagious, especially if you keep more than one horse and use a common watering trough. Symptoms include coughing, discharge from the nose, loss of appetite and possible fever. Keep your horse warm by using a rug or blanket and keeping him out of drafts.

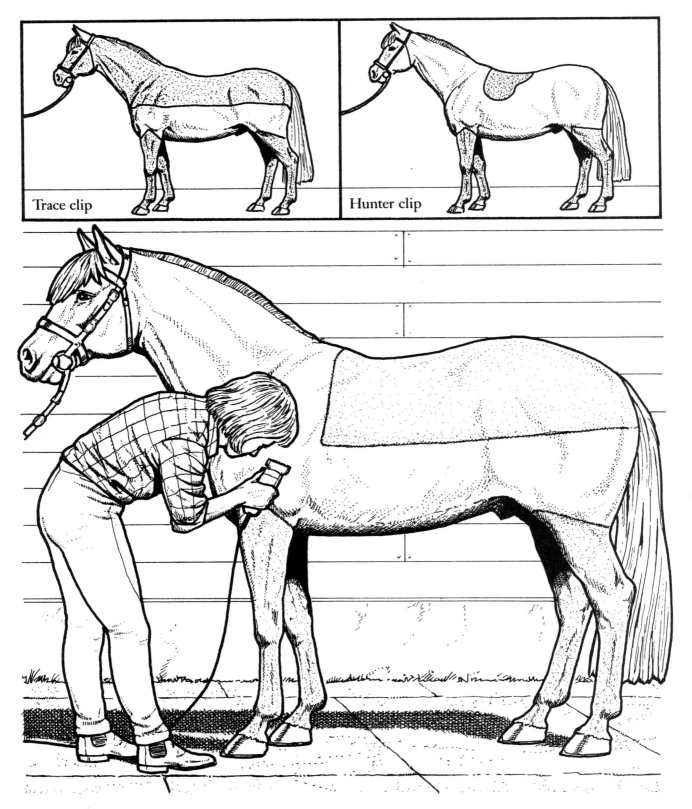

Trace clip

Hunter clip

Clipping the horse. Horses are usually clipped in the fall after their winter coats have grown in. The purpose of clipping is to protect a horse from becoming overheated when exercised. If the horse is not clipped, he will sweat heavily during exercise and the thickness of his winter coat will prevent it from drying out thoroughly. This could result in chills and most likely lead to illness. There are several styles of clipping, as shown here. The main draw-ing illustrates the blanket clip, a style that leaves the coat heavy on the legs and back in the shape of a blanket. This is a cooler clip than the trace clip, shown in the top left drawing. The top right illustration shows the hunter clip, in which the entire coat is clipped except for the legs and a saddle patch; this clip is used for horses that are heavily exercised, as in hunting.

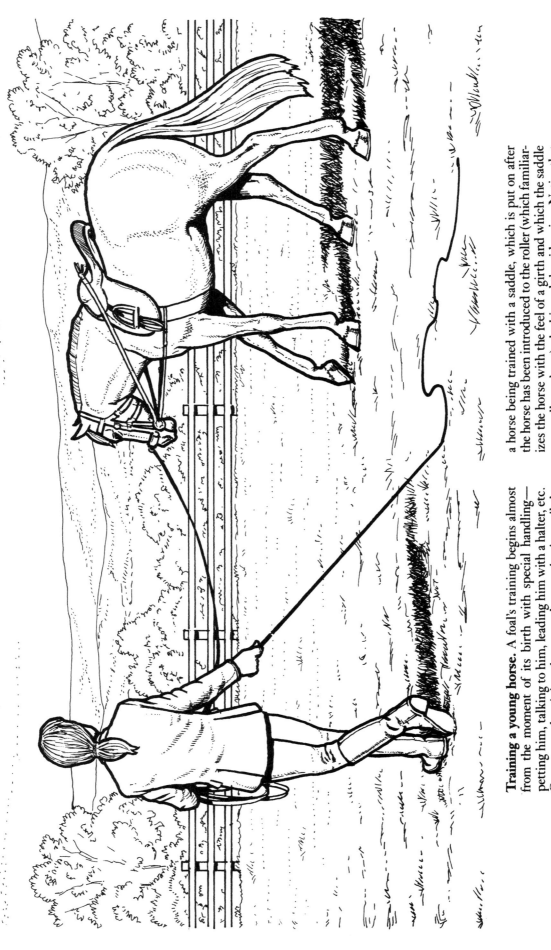

Training a young horse. A foal's training begins almost from the moment of its birth with special handling— petting him, talking to him, leading him with a halter, etc. Concentrated training, however, does not begin until the horse is two to three years old. By this time the horse should be familiar with its trainer and used to obeying basic commands from the halter. Concentrated training begins with the lunge reins and cavesson (a special head-piece with rings for the lunge rein). The illustration shows a horse being trained with a saddle, which is put on after the horse has been introduced to the roller (which familiar-izes the horse with the feel of a girth and which the saddle eventually replaces), the bit and the side reins. Notice that the trainer remains the top point of a triangle formed by the lunge rein, the horse and the whip; by moving the horse in a wide circle, the trainer becomes the center from which the horse takes its commands.

Backing the horse. After the horse has become accustomed to the feel of saddle tack, the next phase in its training is backing. As in all phases, the horse should be introduced gradually to having a rider on its back. Two people are required for this stage of training, the trainer and the rider. With both people talking quietly to the horse to keep him calm, the trainer holds the horse's head while the rider touches the saddle; she then is given a leg up and rests her body over the saddle. Giving the horse time to get accustomed to the weight, the rider then puts her leg over the horse to sit in the saddle. (Notice that the rider's feet are not in the stirrups; this comes later.) Once backing has been completed, the horse's training continues by gradually transferring the center of command from the trainer on the lunge rein to the rider. This is also a good time for the rider to improve her seat and her use of the riding aids.

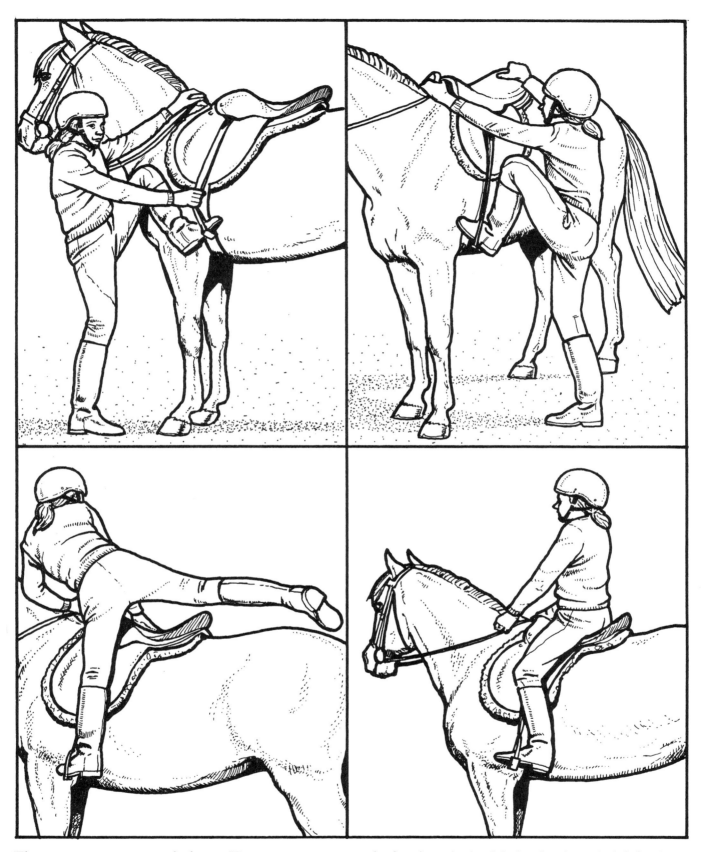

The correct way to mount the horse. The most common way to mount the horse unassisted is illustrated here. Standing at the horse's near, or left, shoulder, hold the reins in the left hand. (These are held short in order to give the rider control over the horse if it tries to back away or circle as the rider attempts to mount.) When the horse is still, take the stirrup in the right hand and put the left foot into it. Using the right hand to grip the saddle, spring up as lightly as possible, bringing the right leg well over the saddle. Once seated, adjust the stirrup leathers and put both feet in the irons.

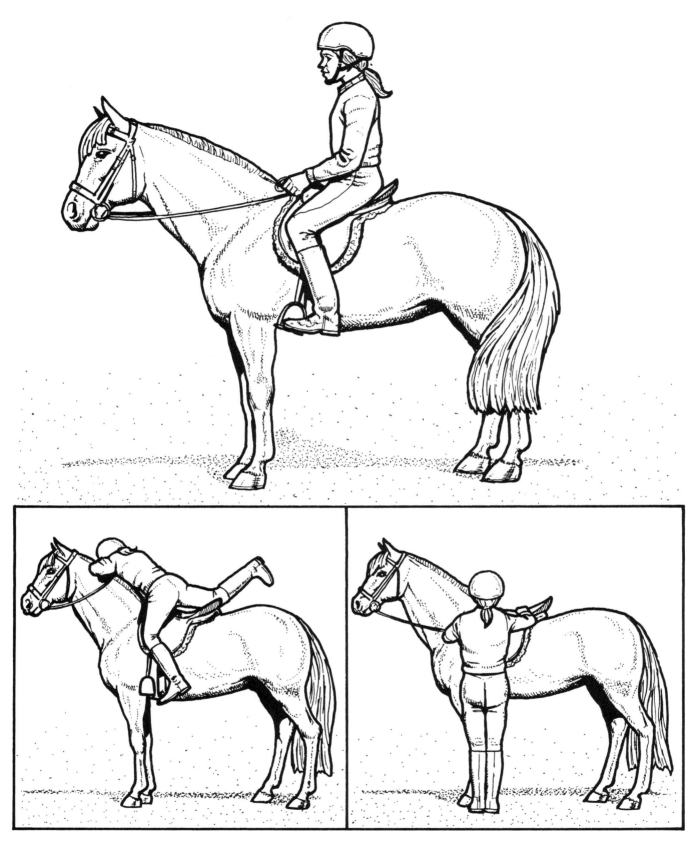

Dismounting. The first step in dismounting is to take your feet out of the stirrups. With the reins in the left hand and the right hand on the pommel of the saddle, shift your weight forward and swing both legs clear of the horse, keeping your weight on the right hand. Drop lightly to the ground, landing on both feet, facing the saddle. Maintain control of the horse by keeping a hold on the reins.

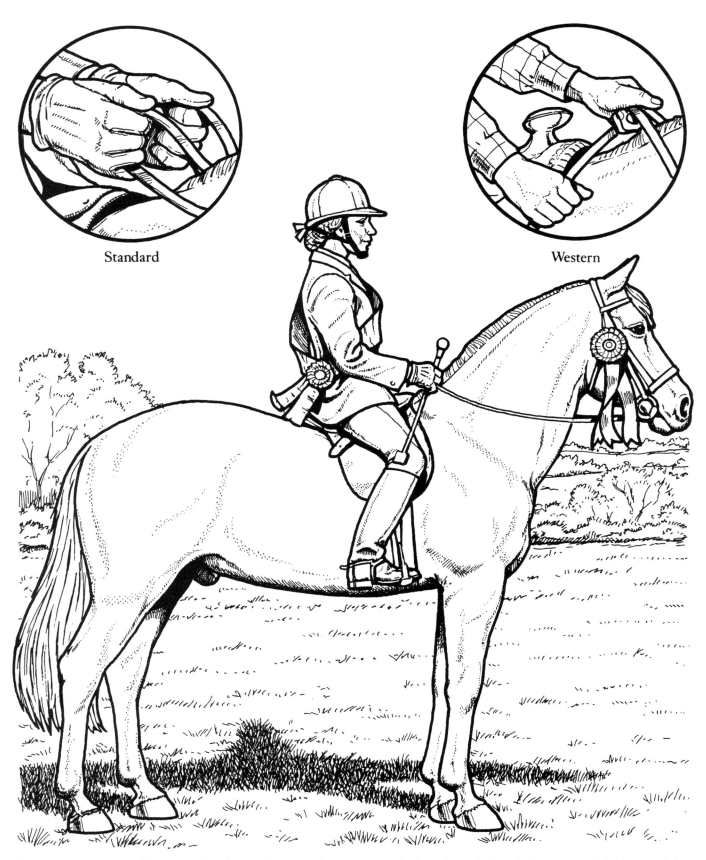

Standard

Western

The correct seat and correct hand positions on the reins. This illustration shows a good seat, the basis for proper riding. As shown here, the rider is well balanced and in control, her seat bones pressed well down in the deepest part of the saddle. The calves are held closely to the horse's side, heels well down. The knees are in line with the toes, the back is straight and the arms are held in a straight line with the reins to the horse's mouth. The hands are held lightly with thumbs uppermost, as shown in the inset of the standard, or English, style. For Western-style riding, the reins are held as shown.

Exercises for the rider. There are several exercises that can be performed on horseback to build the rider's confidence as well as strength. The exercise shown in the top illustration is performed by sitting upright in the saddle with a straight back and outstretched arms. The rider then turns his body from the hips as far as possible in each direction. This exercise develops flexibility of the back and waist. The exercise shown in the bottom left picture is good for strengthening the abdominal muscles. Here the rider leans back and rests her head on the horse's rump for a few moments, then return to the upright position without using the hands or arms; the legs should remain in the riding position. The rider performs the last exercise shown by leaning down and forward over the horse's neck to touch the right toe with the left hand, then vice versa.

Riding aids. There are two kinds of "aids" used to control the horse, natural (shown here) and artificial. The artificial aids are the whip, spurs, martingale (a device that prevents the horse from raising his head far enough to evade the bit) and draw reins. The natural aids—the hands, legs, seat and voice—work in harmony with one another to communicate the rider's commands to her horse. For example, to encourage the horse to move forward, the rider applies pressure from the seat to the horse's hindquarters. The hands operate in a give-and-take manner to maintain a light and steady contact with the horse's mouth. The calves control the pace as well as the direction of the horse.

Walk on

Trot

Canter to trot

Trot to walk

Paces. The most common of the horse's paces are the walk, trot, canter and gallop. All of these gaits are performed by maintaining a proper seat and using the aids correctly. Most work with beginning riders is done at the walk until their confidence has developed, at which time they are ready to go on to the other paces. The transition from a walk to a trot is accomplished by sitting down in the saddle, closing the legs and feeling the inside rein. Once in the trot, the rider can either post (rise slightly out of the saddle for

Canter

Gallop

Halt

Rein back

one beat of the gait) or remain seated deeply in the saddle. Notice that the horse's legs move on the diagonal in the trot. The canter is a three-beat gait in which the horse is not fully extended as he is in the gallop. In this illustration, the rider puts the horse through its paces, from the walk to the gallop and then slows the horse back through from the canter to a halt. The last pace illustrated is reining back, or making the horse move backwards.

Changing direction. As mentioned before, the rider's calves, working with the other aids, control the direction of the horse. To move the horse to the left, the left leg presses on the girth while the right leg is slightly behind its normal position, placed a little behind the girth. The left rein is used as the leading rein, while the right rein is eased; as the horse turns, the rider's upper body turns with it. To go right, the rider presses the horse firmly with the right leg while holding the left leg behind the girth (this prevents the horse's hindquarters from swinging out too far); the right rein leads while the left rein gives. When changing direction, remember to use both the hands and the legs; if only the reins are used, the horse may turn only its head, swinging its hindquarters outwards.

Learning to jump. After a rider has learned the fundamentals of form and control, she can begin learning to jump. Such lessons are very useful in teaching balance and developing the rider's confidence. This illustration shows several of the stages involved when teaching the horse and the rider to jump. For example, a horse untrained in jumping should gradually become accustomed to the task, first being led over poles placed at intervals on the ground. This procedure is repeated at a trot, and then with the rider mounted. Another jumping exercise uses cavalletti, squared-off poles supported at each end by an X-shaped support. Cavalletti can be stacked to form a fence, or placed singly at various intervals on the ground or in other combinations. Schooling both rider and horse over cavalletti develops balance and rhythm.

Types of jumps; homemade jumps. Here we see a variety of homemade jumps, from the post-and-rail jump to one made of hay bales. Notice the rider's position as the horse takes off for the jump: her body is bent forward from the hips, back straight; her head is up, looking in a forward direction and her hands are forward and ready to move down the side of the horse's neck as the horse moves over the jump. Her knees are resting on the saddle and her weight is in her heels. This is the correct forward jumping position.

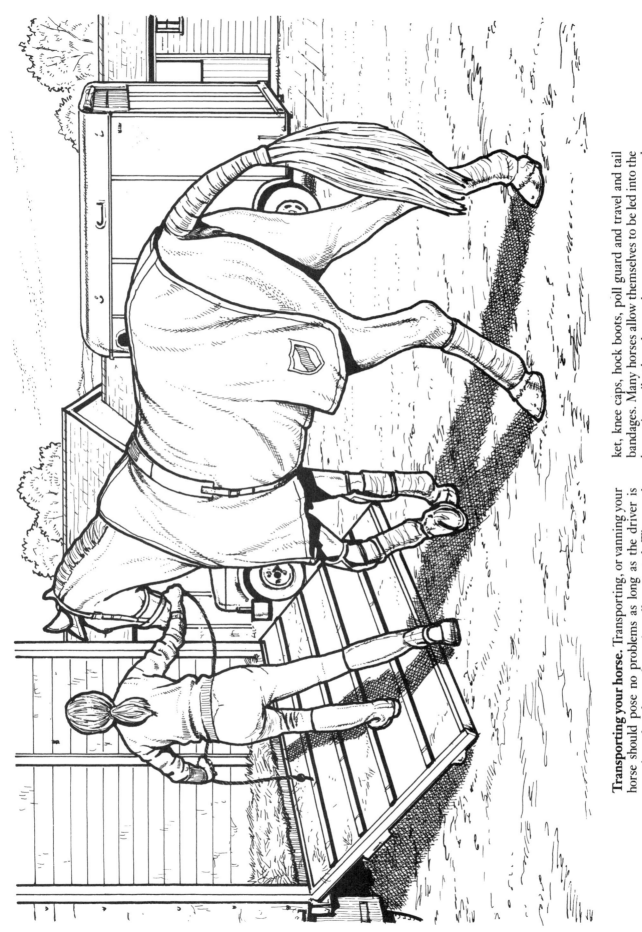

Transporting your horse. Transporting, or vanning your horse should pose no problems as long as the driver is experienced and your horse is well-protected. The usual mode of transportation is the horsebox, the interior of which is padded. In addition, the horse should wear blan-

ket, knee caps, hock boots, poll guard and travel and tail bandages. Many horses allow themselves to be led into the box quite easily, though some horses are more nervous and must be loaded with help. For long journeys, a haynet hung within easy reach can keep horses from becoming restless.

The rodeo. The rodeo (from the Spanish word for a cattle ring) originated in the American West as informal contests of skill held after the big cattle drives. Later formal rodeos were organized with prize money, and today these events attract large numbers of contestants and spectators; there are also professional rodeo organizations such as the Rodeo Cowboys' Association and the Girls' Rodeo Association. There are five traditional rodeo events: bronco riding, saddle bronco riding, bull riding, steer wrestling and calf roping (shown here). In this event, a calf is released into the ring from a chute and the cowboy gallops after to lasso it. Part of the Western horse's basic training is to come to a sliding halt when the calf is roped and to back away, keeping the lariat, which is secured to the horn, taut. The cowboy then dismounts, turns the calf over on its side and ties three of its legs together. The rider who accomplishes this in the least amount of time wins the event.

The horse show and gymkhana. As the rider progresses in horsemanship, it can be both fun and instructive to participate in horse shows and gymkhanas. A gymkhana is a meet in which riders compete in various games or contests, such as the flag race shown here. The word itself is a combined form of "gymnastics" and the Hindustani word for sports ground, "gend-khana." British soldiers serving in India in the nineteenth century brought the idea of such mounted games to the United Kingdom and from there the idea spread throughout the world. Another kind of meet is the horse show, in which horses are judged on performance, appearance and breeding. The most important test for the show horse is conformation, in which the horse's build is judged against the ideal conformation for that horse's breed.

Prize winning, the rodeo and the show. In competitive meets, young riders can reap the rewards of the hard work they put into learning the proper ways to ride and care for their horses. Good horsemanship can instill a sense of confidence, pride and responsibility; it doesn't matter whether the rider takes home first prize or not, as long as she knows she competed and did her best.